THE FRANKENSTEIN JOURNALS

Written by Scott Sonneborn

Stone Arch Books
a Capstone Imprint

The Frankenstein Journals
is published by Stone Arch Books,
A Capstone Imprint
1710 Roe Crest Drive
North Mankato, Minnesota 56003
www.capstonepub.com

I dedicate this journal to my dad.

Cataloging-in-Publication Data is available on the Library of Congress website.
ISBN: 978-1-4342-9000-7 (library hardcover)
ISBN: 978-1-4965-0104-2 (eBook)

Summary: Yep, I'm the son of Frankenstein's Monster. Each body part used to build my dad is like a relative of mine. On this adventure, I'm looking for the relative who gave my dad his EYEBALLS! One day, I'll piece together this whole monster mystery!

Designer: Hilary Wacholz

Illustrated by Timothy Banks

Printed in China by Nordica
0414/CA21400611
032014   008095NORDF14

I for an Eye

Chapter 1

I was standing on the corner of Spring and Second Streets when the whole city of Los Angeles shook!

As the ground RRRRUMBLED, I grabbed the mailbox next to me and wished everything would just stop moving!

And then it did.

That's when I realized I'd just survived my first earthquake. It had only lasted a second or two. It must have been a really small one on the Rictor or Richter or whatever-you-call-it scale.

Nothing was damaged and no one was hurt.

In fact, no one else seemed to notice the earthquake at all. I guess here in Los Angeles, little earthquakes like that one were pretty normal. Everyone around me just kept driving or walking.

The only thing that seemed weird to them was me.

That wasn't too surprising. Anyone who's met me knows I can make a pretty odd first impression.

Maybe it's because my feet are too big for my legs. Or because my left hand is way bigger than my right. Or because one eye is blue and the other is bright green.

Or maybe it's because I'm the son of . . .

FRANKENSTEIN'S MONSTER!

Not that any of the people passing me in downtown Los Angeles knew that. I had only just found that out myself.

I never knew my dad, but I had read about him.
I'd only bothered to print out one of the newspaper
articles I'd found and taped it here in my journal,
because they were all pretty much the same.

Apparently, my dad tended to freak people out.

FRANKENSTEIN'S MONSTER

Some people are scared of genetically modified food. Imagine how they felt meeting a genetically modified MAN!

Actually, I imagined how they felt a lot. I wished I could've traded places with them and met my dad. But he disappeared after leaving me at Mr. Shelley's Orphanage for Lost and Neglected Children® when I was just a baby.

Let's recap, shall we?

No one knew who had left me. So Mr. Shelley, the orphanage director, named me John Doe.

MR. SHELLEY

J.D. for short.

Growing up in the orphanage, the one thing I wanted was a big family. Then one day I found the journal of Dr. Victor Von Frankenstein. I discovered that my dad was Frankenstein's Monster, which meant I had a HUGE family!

Well, kind of.

I inherited my mismatched arms and legs and hands from my dad. The way I figured it, the people he got body parts from were my relatives. I have their hands, feet, and eyes, the same way other kids have their grandmother's ears or their great-uncle's nose.

Those people were probably all dead. (At least, I hoped they had died before Dr. Frankenstein took out parts of their bodies and put them in my dad!)

But those people probably had kids and grandkids. They would be related to me too — they'd be like my cousins!

All I had to do was find out who they were by tracking down where each part of my dad came from.

And I had to find out fast. Because I wasn't the only one looking for my cousins!

Chapter 2

Oops! Sorry. I got a little ahead of myself. I forgot to write down why I had traveled 2,000 miles to Los Angeles in the first place.

It had been a week or so since I had found out my dad was Frankenstein's Monster. So far I had tracked down one cousin. His name was Robert, and he was an explorer whose grandfather's feet had become my dad's feet.

I found him in Antarctica and helped get him out of a tough spot. He was still there now, searching for the woman he was going to marry.

Note to my future Self: If you've forgotten the rest of that story — and I can't believe you ever would — just look back at the earlier part of this journal!

My journal was the most valuable thing I owned. Partly because it was pretty much the only thing I owned. But also because it contained every clue I had found about my cousins.

Taped inside it was every clue I had found about my cousins. Including the pages I had gotten from Dr. Frankenstein's journal.

Dr. F's journal told the story of how he created my dad. I only had copies of a few pages from it, but they were the best clues I had.

After my adventure with Robert, I had gone to stay with his friends at the Explorers Club.

They were so happy I had found Robert, they offered to get me anywhere in the world I wanted to go.

Now I just had to figure out where to go to find my next cousin.

The problem was, I didn't have Dr. Frankenstein's whole journal.

If I had had the whole thing, it would have been a lot easier to figure out where all the parts that went into my dad came from. But the only one who had the whole journal was Fran.

Fran Kenstein (crazy) was Dr. Frankenstein's daughter. She wanted to create a new monster. But there had been something special about the mix of body parts that went into my dad.

To build a new monster, Fran needed body parts with the same DNA. And the only way to get them was to take them from my cousins.

I had beaten her to Robert. Somehow or another, I had to get to the rest of my cousins and warn them about her before she could find them.

Sitting in the library at the Explorers Club, I kept looking at one page from Dr. Frankenstein's journal. It had a detailed drawing of one of my dad's eyes.

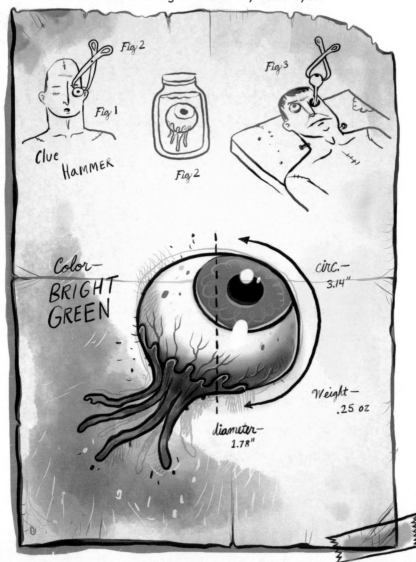

Fig 2

Fig 1

Clue HAMMER

Fig 2

Fig 3

Color— BRIGHT GREEN

circ.— 3.14"

Weight— .25 oz

diameter— 1.78"

But who had Dr. Frankenstein taken it from?

I was sure there had to be a clue on this page. Mostly because the word "clue" was written on it.

"Clue Hammer." What did that mean? Was the hammer a clue? Was a clue hammer what Dr. Frankenstein used to get the eyeball out? (Ew!) Was there even a kind of tool called a "clue hammer"?

GROSS!

Borrowing the explorers' computer, I did a quick search. I learned that there was no such thing as a tool called a clue hammer. But there was a Samuel "Clue" Hammer! He was a famous private detective in Los Angeles in the 1940s.

I wasn't entirely sure what a private detective did. Was it different from being a public detective?

I kept clicking and reading what I found. Turns out, Samuel Hammer held the record for most cases solved in the history of Los Angeles (also, there was no such thing as a public detective).

I found a lot of photos of Samuel Hammer, but since they were from the 1940s, they were in black and white. I couldn't tell if he was the one the bright green eye came from.

Then I found an article from many years later, with a color photo of Samuel holding a baby. Both of them had bright green eyes!

The article didn't say much other than that the famous Samuel Hammer had a newborn grandson.

The only other article that mentioned the grandson was Samuel Hammer's obituary from a years later.

The obituary also mentioned something else: the address and phone number of the detective agency Samuel Hammer worked for! Even though Samuel wasn't around anymore, his office would have records or maybe even someone who had known him! Either way, I'd be able to find his grandson — my cousin!

I raced to the phone, but there was no answer when I called. Maybe everyone in the office was out solving a crime or something.

I put down the phone and ran out the door. It was the only lead I had. And if I had it, there was a good chance Fran had it too.

The explorers had promised to get me anywhere in the world I wanted to go. Now I knew exactly where that was.

Samuel Hammer's office in Los Angeles.

Sixteen hours later, I was crossing Spring Street in downtown LA. Samuel's office was just around the corner. I was so excited, I couldn't help but run the last block to the address. And then I saw it!

I was looking at an empty lot. NOoOOOO!

I had been in such a rush to follow the clue, I hadn't even taken the time to think about it.

Samuel Hammer had been a famous detective in the 1940s. That was like *80* years ago! It shouldn't have been a huge surprise his office wasn't there anymore. That's why no one had answered the phone. The whole building was gone!

"Don't panic," I told myself again. "I'll figure something out."

But the only thing I could think of was "at least things can't get worse."

And then things got worse. Fran Kenstein worse! She was on the other side of the street!

Chapter 3

I ducked into the shadow of the building next door. Fran didn't even glance my way. She was totally focused on where she was going, walking quickly with an evil smile on her face.

I had seen that smile before — when she had talked about taking my cousins' body parts to build her monster!

Was Fran following the same clue from Dr. Frankenstein's journal as I was? Did she know how to find Samuel Hammer's grandson? Was she on her way to him now?

I had to find out.

I trailed her, or tailed her, or whatever you call it as she walked all the way down Grand Avenue. She walked so far that the sun set, and a full moon rose.

OUCH!

My huge feet were aching, but Fran kept walking faster and faster.

Fran marched right up to a building that covered an entire block. Metal letters on top of the building spelled out the words "Los Angeles Convention Center."

Fran pushed her way through a glass door. I counted to three and followed her inside. And ran right into a man-sized badger!

BADGER

There were dozens — no, hundreds — of people-sized animals walking around in there!

Were they victims of one of Fran's insane experiments? What had she done to them?

What would they do to me?

I slowly backed my way toward the door. That's when I saw the banner hanging from the ceiling. It read, "The Los Angeles Convention Center Welcomes You to THE PROFESSIONAL SPORTS MASCOT CONVENTION!"

Okay, whew! These weren't half-human animals. Or even half-animal humans. They were people in mascot costumes! I recognized the dolphin from that football team. And the dinosaur from that basketball team. I wasn't sure what the orange fuzzy thing with the big yellow nose was supposed to be, but I knew I had seen it on TV.

It was actually pretty cool.

Or would have been, if it weren't for Fran.

She still hadn't seen me in the crowd. She was too busy looking for someone else.

Which could only mean one thing . . . One of my cousins was inside one of these mascot costumes!

If Fran was following the same clue from Dr. Frankenstein's journal as I was, she had to be looking for Samuel Hammer's grandson.

But which one was he?

The mascots were covered from head to toe by their costumes. All you could see of the person underneath were their eyes.

Fran looked at costume after costume. But she didn't see what she was looking for. Frustrated, she moved deeper into the sprawling convention center.

And that's when I saw him. He was standing near the men's room, dressed as a grouper. Or maybe a marlin. Definitely some kind of blue fish.

His eyes were focused on a man dressed as a blue jay. Maybe that's what made me notice the bright green in the eyeholes of the fish head.

The same bright green eyes as Samuel Hammer! The same bright **GREEN** as my left eye!

I'd found him!

Now I just had to make sure Fran didn't.

As soon as Fran was out of sight, I raced up to my cousin.

I didn't know how long I had before Fran wandered back. I had to warn him now.

"There's something I've got to tell you right away," I said. "You're the grandson of Samuel Hammer, the famous detective, right?"

"Shh! Quiet!" whispered the man in the fish costume. "Did the Chief send you?"

"Chief?" I asked, confused. "Wait, you mean that Indian Chief mascot over there? No, I . . . well, this is kind of hard to explain, but my name's J.D. and —"

"Look, that's swell. But can you scram?" he replied. "Don't mean to give you the bum's rush, but I'm kind of busy here."

"Actually, no," I told him. "This can't wait. See, there's this girl named Fran Kenstein who is hunting for my cousins. So if you're the grandson of Samuel Hammer, the famous detective —"

"Detective? Who's a detective?!" cried a man dressed in a blue jay costume. He had been about to go into the men's room. Instead, he took off running for the exit.

"Thanks, kid!" sighed my cousin.

"You're welcome," I replied.

"No, I meant everything's all wet because of you!" he exclaimed. "I'm a detective, just like my granddad. And I'm undercover on a case! I was following that guy in the blue jay costume!"

"Oh," was all I could think to say.

The detective reached inside his fish costume and pulled out a police walkie-talkie.

"All units near the convention center, this is Detective Sam Hammer of the MCU! Requesting backup! Suspect on the run!" he said into his walkie-talkie. "Suspect is approximately six feet tall and dressed as a blue jay. Over!"

The detective put his walkie-talkie down and slipped out of his costume. "The two-time loser inside that blue jay costume is a hood named Lavenza," he said to me. "I've been tailing him for days. Lavenza's a thug for hire. Big-time crooks call him when they are planning some very bad business. He was just pretending to be a mascot to meet the criminal who wanted to hire him."

The detective looked at the bathroom Lavenza had been about to enter. "Which means that palooka is probably in there!"

The detective put his hand on the bathroom door. "Stay out here," he warned me. "It could get dangerous in there."

He was right. Only the danger didn't stay inside!

A man in a wolf costume slashed through the door with his claws!

He knocked the detective over.

And then he ran right at **ME!!**

CREEPY!

Chapter 4

All I saw was hair.

The man running at me was covered in it. He was so furry, the hair covered the blue suit with square buttons that he was wearing. He raced right past me and disappeared into the crowd.

"Are you okay?" the detective asked.

"Yeah," I nodded. "I don't know how he could move so fast in that costume."

"Hooey! That was no costume," he said. "Could costume claws do this?"

The detective pointed to the bathroom door — or what was left of it. It was shredded.

"That," said the detective, "was the Werewolf! I've been trying to bust that mug for months. Now shake a leg! We gotta catch him!"

He grabbed my big left hand and dragged me into the crowd after him.

"We?" I asked. "I'm no detective! I don't know the first thing about detecting. Wait, is that even a word? See! I don't even know that."

"I didn't get a look at him, kid," said the detective. "I'll need you to help me spot him."

"Um, don't you think a hairy Werewolf will kind of stand out in a crowd?" I asked as I tried to keep up with him.

"In this crowd?" he replied. "No dice."

The convention floor was packed with hundreds of people dressed as lions, tigers, and every other animal you could think of.

Including wolves. RRRRR!

It was probably the only place on the planet the Werewolf could walk around without being noticed. Which must have been why he picked it.

"My name's Sam, by the way," said the detective as we ran past penguins, sharks, and falcons, looking for the Werewolf. "Sam Hammer the Third. Say, how'd you know I was here undercover?"

"I didn't," I told him. "I just recognized your bright green eyes."

"You got the eye of a detective, kid," he said, impressed. "And I should know. I inherited mine from my grandfather."

"I think I inherited mine from him too," I replied.

As we made our way through the crowd, I told him my story. I took out my journal and showed him the drawing of his grandfather's eye. Which went into my dad. Which made us related.

Sam didn't even bat a green eye. "When you put it like that, I guess that does make us related," he said. "I'm not surprised. You definitely followed the clues to me like a born detective."

"I don't know about that. I'm just lucky I found you," I told him. "I knew about your grandfather, but there was hardly anything online about you."

Sam's face turned red.

"That's because I haven't cracked any cases big enough to get in the papers," he said. "Not yet. But I will. I learned everything I know about being a gumshoe from my granddad. Including how to flap my gums."

"Flap your gums?" I asked.

Sam shrugged. "That's how detectives in the 1940s used to say 'talk,'" he told me. "And if it was good enough for my granddad, it's swell enough for me."

I didn't ask him why people in the 1940s said "flap your gums" when it was a lot easier just to say "talk." It was probably the same reason people in the Middle Ages said "thou" instead of "you." Or why people used to ride horses instead of cars.

People a long time ago just liked to do really strange stuff.

"No gumshoe in this city of angels ever cracked more cases than my granddad did," said Sam. "I've spent my whole life trying to be as great a detective as he was. And until I do, I'm not gonna stop!"

And then he stopped.

We had reached the end of the convention center. There was no sign of the Werewolf.

Sam took out his walkie-talkie.

"This is Detective Hammer of the MCU," he shouted into the walkie-talkie. "I'm in pursuit of the second suspect. He may have left the building. All units, be on the lookout for the Werewolf. Description — hair: long. Claws: sharp."

Then Sam saw something through the crowd. His face went white.

"What is it?" I asked. "Is it the Werewolf?"

"No dice. It's much worse than that," said Sam. "It's my boss."

Chapter 5

The Chief of Police marched up. He was followed by several policemen. They had the man in the blue jay costume in tow.

"Let me do the gum flapping," Sam told me. "You take that notebook or journal or whatever it is in your back pocket and draw the Werewolf. You had the best look at him. I want you to draw as many details before you forget them."

The Chief's dress uniform was blue. His gloves were white. His face was red. A very angry red.

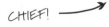

CHIEF! ⟶

"I can explain, Chief," Sam started.

"No!" roared the Chief. "I'm going to explain something to YOU! I shouldn't have to remind you of this, but you're a detective in the MCU," roared the Chief. "That stands for the Monster Crimes Unit! That means you're supposed to investigate monster crimes. You know, crimes committed by the Mummy or the Vampire — guys like that."

Holy crud!

monster crimes!

Did that mean Sam had run into my dad?

Now didn't seem like a good time to ask. Sam was too busy being yelled at by the Chief.

"Lavenza is not a monster!" the Chief shouted as he pointed at the man in the blue jay costume. "He's just a crook in a silly bird costume. And it's not even a monster costume! That means it's not your job to go after him!"

Then the Chief turned to the police officers holding Lavenza. "Take him back to headquarters and put him in a cell. I'll figure out what to do with him later."

The policemen took Lavenza away, leaving the Chief behind.

"But this was a monster crime, sir," Sam insisted. "Lavenza only works for criminals who are planning big crimes. And he was here to meet the Werewolf! They're in cahoots!"

The Chief groaned. "Here we go again with the Werewolf! You've been talking about him for months! But you've never been able to find a single shred of evidence that he even exists."

"I know, but this time I've got an eyewitness who got a good look at him!" Sam said. "J.D., show the Chief what you saw."

I handed the Chief my journal, open to the page where I had drawn the Werewolf.

The Chief studied the picture. "Oh, okay, now I see," he said. Then he roared, "I see a child's drawing of some guy covered in fur. Which describes pretty much everyone here! You probably just saw someone in a wolf costume.

"Look, Sam," said the Chief in a gentler voice, "I know how important it is to you to live up to your grandfather's legend. He was a great detective. The greatest, in fact. But this isn't your case. Because it's not a monster crime. If Lavenza was here to meet another criminal, leave it to the regular cops to figure out who it was."

"Actually," said a voice from the crowd. "You don't have to leave it to anyone. I can tell you exactly who it was."

Oh, no — I recognized that voice. It was Fran! She smiled as she walked up to the Chief.

"Don't listen to her!" I told the Chief.   UGH!

"I give orders. I don't take them!" scowled the Chief. "Now what are you talking about?" he asked Fran.

"That peculiar-looking boy!" said Fran, pointing at me. "He must be a criminal! I saw him with the man in the blue jay costume. They were talking together. It looked like they were plotting something!"

"Is that so?" said the Chief, turning to me.

"NO, IT'S NOT!" I said.

"I trust the boy, Chief," Sam insisted.

"And why is that?" asked the Chief. "Do you know him?"

"Yes," Sam said. "Well, we just met a few minutes ago. But he's my cousin. Well, not technically. But —"

"I see," interrupted the Chief. He turned to me. "What's your name?" the Chief asked.

"J.D.," I stammered.

"Last name?" he asked.

"It's just J.D.," I told him. "It stands for John Doe."

"I see," he scowled. "And what is your address?"

"Well, since I left the orphanage, I don't exactly have one," I admitted.

"Hmm . . . a John Doe with no known address," the Chief said to Sam. "And that doesn't sound at all suspicious?"

"Well, I can see how that might sound a little hinky," Sam admitted.

The Chief turned to Fran. "Thank you for coming forward," the Chief told her.

"Only too happy to help," she beamed.

"Wait, you can't believe what she says!" I said. "You don't know who she is!"

"My name is Fran Kenstein," Fran told the Chief.

Fran held out her wallet. "Here is my ID with my address."

"Now I know who SHE is," the Chief said to me, "which is more than I can say for you, John Doe with no known address.

"You see, Sam?" the Chief told Sam. "Just like I told you, this isn't a case for the Monster Crimes Unit. Lavenza was here to meet this kid! But I'll tell you what. Since you're so eager to be involved, I'll let you bring the boy back to HQ so he can be processed."

Something bounced against the inside of my shirt. I looked down and realized it was my heart! I was going to jail!

YIKES!

How could the Chief believe Fran? If he only knew what she was really like . . .

But of course he didn't. Only I did. Well, Fran did too. But she wasn't telling.

"I would take him in myself," the Chief continued, "but I'm late for a haircut. When I get back, I want to see him in a cell!"

CHOP
CHOP

"But Chief —" Sam started.

"The only thing I want to hear from you is 'Yes, sir!'" barked the Chief. "I don't care if your grandfather was Samuel Hammer. If you don't follow my orders, I'll make sure you never work as a detective in Los Angeles again!"

Sam's face went white. "Yes, sir," he mumbled.

"Good," said the Chief. Then he turned to Fran. "Thank you again for your time."

"It was my pleasure." She smiled.

"I had been in a hurry to visit someone," she said as she looked at Sam. Then she turned to me and added darkly: "Actually several someones. But it looks like I now have all the time in the world to do that. There won't be anything getting in my way anymore."

I tried to think of something to say to her. But it was kind of hard to think when Sam was CLICKING handcuffs around my wrists.

The Chief nodded to Sam, then escorted Fran out of the building.

"Okay," I told myself. "Don't panic. You'll think of something."

And, you know what, I did think of something.

I thought, "I AM SO DOOMED!"

Chapter 6

"You can't do this!" I pleaded with Sam. "If I'm locked up, who is going to warn my other cousins about Fran?"

"You heard what the Chief said," said Sam.

And then he unlocked my cuffs! HUH?!?!

"The Chief said he expects to see you behind bars when he gets back to the office," said the detective. "So I'd say that gives us two hours tops to pinch the Werewolf and prove the Chief gave you a bum rap. So let's shake a leg!"

Sam led me back to the bathroom door the Werewolf had shredded.

"What a bunch of hooey!" Sam said, shaking his head. "The Chief is so sure you were the one meeting Lavenza, he didn't leave anyone to search for clues the Werewolf might have left. That means it's up to us, J.D.!"

I followed Sam as he went into the bathroom and started looking around.

"I don't know why the Chief didn't believe me." Sam sighed. "But he's always looked down on the Monster Crimes Unit."

"Oh, man! In all the excitement about going to jail and my life being over, I totally forgot! You're in the Monster Crimes Unit!" I said. "That means you know all about monsters!"

"MONSTERS LIKE MY DAD!"

"Well, yes and no," said Sam as he searched the bathroom for clues. "Frankenstein's Monster disappeared years before I became a gumshoe. But that doesn't mean I can't help you find out about him. As soon as we pinch the Werewolf, I promise, I'll — holy mazuma!"

Sam had been digging through the trash can next to the sink. Now he started digging even faster. "I found something!" he exclaimed. "Look!"

In Sam's hands were ripped-up pieces of paper.

"You found some trash in the trash can? What's so strange about that?" I asked.

"This isn't trash. It's a clue! A really swell clue! This paper wasn't ripped. It was shredded. See the cut marks on the edges? You'll find the same marks on the door," he said. "Because they were both shredded by the Werewolf's claws!"

I looked. He was right!

"The Werewolf must have tried to destroy this when he heard us outside," Sam said as he collected more pieces of paper. "Now let's put this back together and see what it says!"

We got to work piecing the paper back together. Unfortunately, it turned out werewolf claws were really good at shredding! We couldn't find all the pieces, but we taped what we found onto a page in my journal (good thing I kept some tape — as well as a couple of pens — in my back pocket with my journal).

"There's a lot missing, but these are definitely instructions for the crime the Werewolf's plotting tonight!" said Sam. "He must have been planning to give this to Lavenza. But he never got the chance!

"And look at this," said Sam, pointing to what looked like part of a necklace of circles at the top of the page. "That symbol looks familiar. I can't remember where I've seen it, though. Somewhere back at HQ. Maybe in the Werewolf's police file."

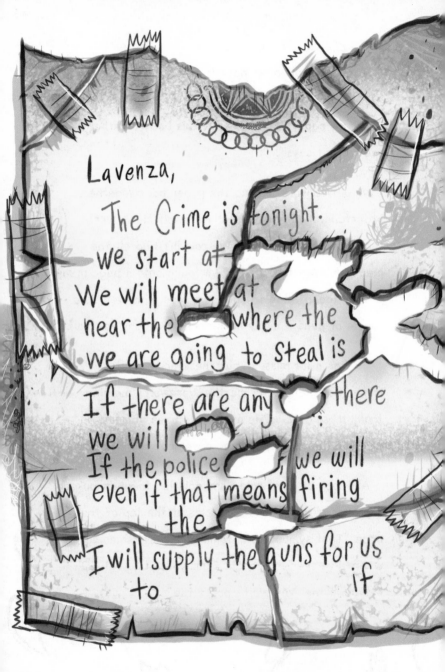

Lavenza,

The Crime is tonight.
we start at
We will meet at
near the   where the
we are going to steal is

If there are any   there
we will
If the police   , we will
even if that means firing
the

I will supply the guns for us
to   if

46

"Then let's go! We gotta show this to the Chief of Police," I exclaimed excitedly. "It proves the Werewolf was the one Lavenza was here to meet."

Sam shook his head. "I don't see where this is signed by the Werewolf, do you?" he asked. "In fact, This doesn't prove squat. Anyone could have written this including you, J.D.

"At least, that's what the Chief of Police would say," he finished.

I slumped. We were no closer to figuring this out than when we started!

"Just because a clue doesn't tell you everything doesn't mean it's telling you nothing," Sam said. "Sometimes, a sleuth just needs someone to give him a little more information to put the puzzle together."

"That's great," I replied. "But who's going to give us more information?"

"The Werewolf," Sam said with a smile.

 — NO WAY!

Chapter 7

Sam led me through the convention center to a room marked "Video Surveillance."

Sam showed his badge to the man inside. He left and Sam sat down at the controls in front of a big monitor.

"I'm pulling up the footage from when we saw the Werewolf," Sam told me. "That's going to take a minute or two."

While I waited, I took out my journal and thought of everyone on the Chief's list of suspects.

Lavenza. Me.

That right there was my problem: how was I going to get my name off that list and the real criminal's name on it?

Of course, there was one easy way to do that. I took out my pen and wrote:

That didn't really change anything. Well, not true — it did change one thing. It made me feel a little better. Just a little.

Sam saw what I had written.

"That should be Werewolf," said Sam. "Not Wolfman."

"What's the difference?" I asked.

"Well, for starters, a Wolfman is a man," said Sam. "We don't know if the Werewolf is a guy or a dame. Even if it is a he, he could be anybody."

"Or anywhere," I sighed.

"That's what we are here to narrow down," said Sam. "Take a look at these."

Sam laid out a bunch of printouts from the convention center's main surveillance camera.

They all looked pretty much the same to me: they each showed the entire convention floor crowded with sports mascots.

The only difference was the time printed on the bottom of the photos.

"This camera takes a photo of the entire convention floor every sixty seconds. These were taken from the time the Werewolf ran from us until now," Sam explained. "If we can see which exit he ankled out of, it may give us a clue as to where he went."

I nodded and took half of the stack of pictures to look through. Each one had dozens of furry costumed mascots.

Looking for the Werewolf in that crowd was like trying to find a needle in a furstack.

So I was pretty surprised when I spotted him (or maybe her?) right away!

"Aces!" Sam smiled. "You really do have the eye of a gumshoe! There's the Werewolf, right there, going into that bathroom right in the middle of the convention center!

"What is it with the Werewolf and bathrooms?" Sam wondered, trying to figure out if it were some kind of clue.

"Maybe he isn't housebroken?" I offered.

Sam didn't answer. He was busy shuffling through the rest of the printouts.

DON'T FORGET TO FLUSH

"Look at this," said Sam. "This is the picture taken a minute later. There's the Chief already here, pretty close to where the Werewolf was in your photo. If the Werewolf had left the bathroom then, the Chief would have seen him for sure."

Sam pulled out the rest of the photos and looked through them quickly. There was no sign of the Werewolf in any of them.

"Which means," said Sam, "the Werewolf never came out of that bathroom!"

A minute later, Sam and I were standing outside of that bathroom.

"This could get pretty hairy," Sam said. "Better let me go first."

I didn't argue with that.

Sam charged in. It was hairy, all right. Very hairy!

There was hair everywhere in the bathroom.

But there was no Werewolf. Or anyone else. The bathroom was empty, except for the fur everywhere.

And the disposable razor and can of shaving cream on the sink.

"Of course!" said Sam as he picked up the shaving cream. "We never saw the Werewolf come out of the bathroom because he shaved off all his hair!

"But that would leave him naked," Sam continued, thinking it through. "Unless he had clothes somewhere . . ."

"He had clothes," I said, thinking, "when he ran past me. Under all his hair he was wearing some kind of blue suit."

"That answers that," Sam nodded. "He'd still have his claws, though. But he could easily have hidden them in his pockets. Or in a pair of gloves.

"In which case," Sam continued, "the Werewolf would have come out of here looking like he normally does. And since we don't know what that looks like, this is a —"

"Dead end." I sighed.

OH CRUD!

Chapter 8

"Good gumshoes don't let dead ends stop them," said Sam. "When they hit one, they change directions and keep going."

"How are we supposed to keep going?" I asked. "We don't know where to go!"

"We don't know where the Werewolf is," Sam said, "but there's one hood we do know where to find."

I smiled. "Lavenza!" The Chief had told the policemen to take him back to headquarters and put him in a cell.

"If we get him to sing," Sam said, nodding, "he may be the one to piece this puzzle together!"

The Los Angeles Police Department headquarters was cube-shaped building of glittering glass.

Most boys my age would have been psyched to have been personally invited there by the Chief of Police.

Of course, my invitation was more like a one-way ticket. Which actually turned out to be a good thing.

When the officers at the front desk asked what I was doing there, Sam told them the Chief had ordered him to take me to the holding cells.

By the looks on their faces, I could tell most of them were too scared of the Chief to call and ask him. But if any of them did, the Chief would have told them that Sam was telling the truth.

So that was one good thing about the Chief wanting me locked up, I guess.

"Watch your beezer," Sam warned as we walked down the hallway toward the holding cells.

"Got it," I nodded back. Then I whispered, "Wait, my beezer is my back right?"

"Nope, your nose," Sam said.

"That was totally my next guess," I lied.

Lavenza was sitting in his cell, still wearing his blue jay costume.

← JAILBIRD! HA!

"All right, jailbird," said Sam. "I need you to sing."

Lavenza leaped up. "Sure!" He nodded eagerly. "I'll tell you anything I know. I don't like jail. I just want to get out of here!"

"Swell," said Sam. "So look here, we found the note the Werewolf was going to give you —"

"Wait, the Werewolf?" interrupted Lavenza. "Was that who was trying to hire me? I only talked to him once on the phone. I never got to meet him." Lavenza looked at me. "That kid blew your cover, and I ran before I could."

"Never mind that," said Sam. "I want to know about the Werewolf's plan. Spill!"

"I can't!" moaned Lavenza.

"Don't be a sap," Sam told him. "Don't you want out of here?"

"I do!" cried Lavenza. "But I can't tell you his plan, because I don't know what he was planning! All I know is I got a call from some guy, asking me to help him pull some big crime. I didn't know it was the Werewolf. He told me to rent this costume and meet him at the mascot convention so he could fill me in on the crime.

"But I never got to meet him," he wailed. "Because of you!"

Sam turned to me. He didn't say it, but I knew what he was thinking.

Another dead end.

DEAD END

← NOT AGAIN!

We were running out of leads — and out of time. In fact, we were down to our very last lead: that necklace of circles on the top of the note the Werewolf had written for Lavenza.

Sam told me to wait in the detective's lunchroom while he got the Werewolf's file to see if that's where he had seen that symbol before.

"At this time of night, no one should come in here," he said as he left me in the bathroom. "But just in case, lock the door until I come back."

As I waited for Sam, I took out my journal and started writing down what had happened. I didn't get very far before there was a light knock at the door. Sam was back, carrying two thick folders.

"Here's the file on the Werewolf," said Sam, patting the folder he held under one arm. "And here's one for you," he said, tossing another file on the table.

Sam went to a vending machine and threw in a handful of quarters. He offered me half of what came out of the slot, but I shook my head.

EWW!

I was hungry, but not hungry enough to eat a stale avocado sandwich.

Not when I had the LAPD's file on Frankenstein's Monster sitting on the table in front of me!

Inside could be the answer to every question I ever had about my dad!

And maybe a whole bunch of clues to finding my other cousins!

"Like I said, your dad was before my time," Sam told me as he crunched loudly on his sandwich. "But in that file is everything the police ever found out about him."

I opened the file to the cover page.

But before I could get any farther, Sam cried out: "You gotta be kidding me! What a load of bunk!

"There's nothing in the Werewolf's file!" he exclaimed. "Look! It's just stuffed with blank pages! Someone took everything out!"

"Maybe it was another detective in the Monster Crimes Unit?" I suggested. "Maybe he took it to the copy machine or something?"

Sam shook his head. "I'm the only detective in the Monster Crimes Unit. And if the Chief had his way, there wouldn't even be me."

"So then who could have taken it?" I asked.

"I don't know, kid," he said. "Detectives aren't allowed to touch files that aren't in their department. Not without special permission from someone way high up."

I turned back to my dad's file.

If I was going to jail, at least I could go with answers to all my questions about him. But I didn't get past the cover page.

Because I saw it!

What we had been looking for was right there!

In the middle of the cover sheet was the LAPD logo.

JUN 9. 93

AUG 2. 56

MONSTER CRIMES UNIT

CONFIDENTIAL

FRANKENSTEIN'S MONSTER

LAPD

OCT

RESTRICTED MATERIAL

MAR 22. 04

DEC 11. 77

If you covered up the top two-thirds of the logo, the bottom part that was left looked exactly like the "necklace" of circles we had seen on the note the Werewolf had shredded!

Sam slapped his forehead. "Of course!" he cried. "I can't believe I didn't recognize it! I had been trying to think of what criminal organization had a symbol like that. I never would have thought of something I see every day!"

Something BUZZED loudly.

"Hang on," Sam said. "I'm getting a call on my blower." He took out his walkie-talkie and hit a button.

A voice roared out the speaker: "Why isn't that kid behind bars?" shouted the Chief.

Chapter 9

Sam and I stood in the Chief's office, waiting for him to come out of his private bathroom.

And for life as I knew it to end.

As we stood there, I looked around. I guess I thought the Chief of Police would have had a fancy office, like a President or a CEO. But there actually wasn't much in it. Just a desk, a comfy chair, and a wastebasket.

Which was filled with disposable razors and empty cans of shaving cream!

The same kind we had found in the convention center bathroom where the Werewolf . . .

No. No Way!

That's when I noticed the Chief's blue uniform jacket hanging on a hook on the outside of the bathroom door.

It was the exact same blue as the suit I had seen under the Werewolf's fur.

The Chief's jacket was decorated with several medals. SQUARE medals. Which looked just like what I had thought were square buttons on the Werewolf's jacket!

Hang on. The Chief was the Werewolf?

If he were, it would explain why the note to Lavenza was written on paper with the police logo on it! And why when the Werewolf went into the convention center bathroom and shaved, we saw the Chief outside the bathroom a minute later!

Not to mention, the Chief was in the bathroom again right now! Which was like the Werewolf's favorite place to be!

"Sam!" I whispered. "You're not going to believe it, but I think —"

And that's when the door to the bathroom opened.

I clammed up fast.  ← HA!

As the Chief came out, I saw another disposable razor on the sink behind him. And there was a tuft of thick fur on the back of his neck! He had missed a spot with his razor!

There was no doubt about it. The Chief was the Werewolf.

And we were trapped in his office with him!

I couldn't risk saying anything to Sam. Not without at least letting the Chief know that I knew who he was first!

"This is not going to end well for you," the Chief growled at me.

Oh no! I waited for him to say "Because I know you know!" and then leap at me!

But instead he said, "Because you're about to go to jail for a long time."

Whew! I didn't think anyone had ever felt so relieved to hear they were going to jail!

"Chief, wait," said Sam.

"You're in enough trouble as it is, Detective! That boy should already be behind bars," said the Chief as he pointed a white-gloved finger at me.

Now that I knew what to look for, I could see there was something wrong about his fingers inside his white gloves. Because they weren't fingers at all.

They were claws!

"Sam, I'm really ready to go to jail right now!" I cried.

"Good," said the Chief. "Take him now, Sam. I've got somewhere I have to be."

The Chief got up to leave. Oh, crud! He must have been leaving to commit his crime!

I just wanted to get out of his office without the Chief turning his claws on me.

But the note he wrote to Lavenza said people might get hurt. Maybe even killed. I had to do something.

Maybe there was a way I could figure out what the Chief was planning to do. Without him figuring out what I was trying to do! Then I could fill Sam in when we were safely out of the Chief's reach. I didn't know if it would work, but I had to try.

So I turned to the Chief and tried to sound normal as I asked, "So, um, where are you off to?"

WOW!

One of the Chief's bushy eyebrows moved an inch up his forehead. "Why would you want to know that?" he asked.

Well, because the shredded note said the Werewolf was going to strike tonight, but it didn't say where! But I couldn't tell the Chief that! Or else he'd surely shred me too!

"Go on, J.D.," Sam told me. "Answer the Chief."

Oh man! I guess Sam hadn't figured the Chief was the Werewolf!

"Show him your journal," said Sam, as he grabbed it out of my pocket. "Show him the surveillance photos from the convention center. The one that shows the Werewolf going into a bathroom and the other that shows the Chief showing up a minute later. Tell him how we found shaving cream and a razor in that bathroom. And how the Werewolf's file is gone, even though very few people have access to it."

Sam put my journal in my terror-frozen hands.
Then he flipped through the pages, showing the
Chief everything we had found.

"Oh, I'm sure the Chief doesn't want to see all this,"
I said nervously.

"Actually, I do," said the Chief, taking off his gloves.

"Sam, run!" I cried. "The Chief is the Werewolf!

"So you figured it out!" he roared as he
leaped and blocked the door.
"Nice detective work." Then he
flashed his claws! "Not that it'll
do you any good!"

"Maybe not," said Sam. "But I think this will."

Sam held up his walkie-talkie, showing the Chief it
had been on the whole time. The rest of the police
department must have heard everything!

Sam had already known the Chief was the
Werewolf. Figures. We were related, after all.

"RRRRRRR!" the Chief roared angrily.

He leaped across his desk and swung a huge claw right at my chest.

Just as it was about to hit . . .

RRRRRRRUMMBLE! The room shook!

It was another earthquake!

It only lasted a second, but that was long enough to throw off the Chief's swing!

And that's when the police burst in with their guns drawn! The Chief put his clawed hands up.

Sam rushed over to where I had fallen on the ground. The Chief's claws had missed my chest, but they'd still hit something vital.

My journal! I'd lost a few pages. But better them than me!

It took a dozen policemen to drag the Chief away. Even more showed up to slap Sam on the back. He was a hero!

They all told Sam they had had hunches that the Chief was no good. But it was Sam who had finally proven that to be true.

Sam left with them to take my journal (which was now evidence) to be processed. I spent a few minutes waiting in the Chief's empty office.

Pretty quickly, a police officer came and handed me my journal. He slapped me on my back (I guess back-slapping is something police officers like to do?) and thanked me for helping Sam discover that the Chief was the Werewolf. He assured me I was no longer a suspect and that I was free to go.

I wanted to say goodbye to Sam. But the officer made it clear Sam was busy making sure the Chief stayed behind bars for good and that I should get going.

So I left police HQ. As I did, something fell out of my journal.

It was a note. From Sam!

J.D. —

Sorry for the bum's rush, but I had to get you out of there quick. If you had stayed, you would have had to make a statement and stick around to testify against the Chief. And I know you don't have time for that. You've got to shake a leg and find the rest of your cousins.

Your cousins are lucky to have you on the case. It took me until now to finally solve a mystery worthy of Samuel Hammer. You did it on the first try! But I guess I shouldn't be surprised. Because you've got the same detective's eye as my grandfather.

As soon as I make sure the Chief is locked up in the big house for good, I'll come and help you. In the meantime, I put something else in your journal to keep you busy.

Your cousin,

Sam

I saw that Sam had stuffed something else in my journal. The pages from my dad's police file!

There were probably a ton of clues in there that would lead me to the rest of my cousins!

I was psyched. If this had been the end of my story, it totally would have been a happy ending.

But that's not the way life works.

It keeps going and going. If you're lucky.

I had a lot of cousins out there who might not be so lucky. Unless I figured out where the rest of my dad's body parts came from. Fast!

And that was just what I was going to do!

THE END?

GLOSSARY

disposable (diss-POH-zuh-buhl) — made to be thrown away after use

DNA (dee en AY) — the molecule that carries the genetic code that gives living things their special characteristics

escorted (ess-KOR-tuhd) — accompanied someone, especially to protect the person

impression (im-PRESH-uhn) — to have a strong effect on someone

neglected (ni-GLEK-tuhd) — failed to take care of someone or something

obituary (oh-BICH-oo-wer-ee) — a notice of a person's death, which is usually published in a newspaper

orphanage (OR-fuh-nij) — a place where orphans live and are looked after

testify (TESS-tuh-fye) — to state the truth, or to give evidence in a court of law

77

NOT AS SCARY AS HE LOOKS!

Scott Sonneborn has written dozens of books, one circus (for Ringling Bros. and Barnum & Bailey), and a bunch of TV shows. He's been nominated for one Emmy and spent three very cool years working at DC Comics. He lives in Los Angeles with his wife and their two sons.

COOLEST ILLUSTRATOR EVER!

Timothy Banks is an award-winning illustrator known for his ability to create magically quirky illustrations for kids and adults. He has a Master of Fine Arts degree in Illustration from the Savannah College of Art & Design, and he also teaches fledgling art students in his spare time. Timothy lives in Charleston, SC, with his wonderful wife, two beautiful daughters, and two crazy pugs.

Find a **MONSTER** load of fun at...

WWW.CAPSTONEKIDS.COM

Find cool websites and more books like this one at
www.Facthound.com. Just type in the BOOK I.D:
9781434290007 and your ready to go!

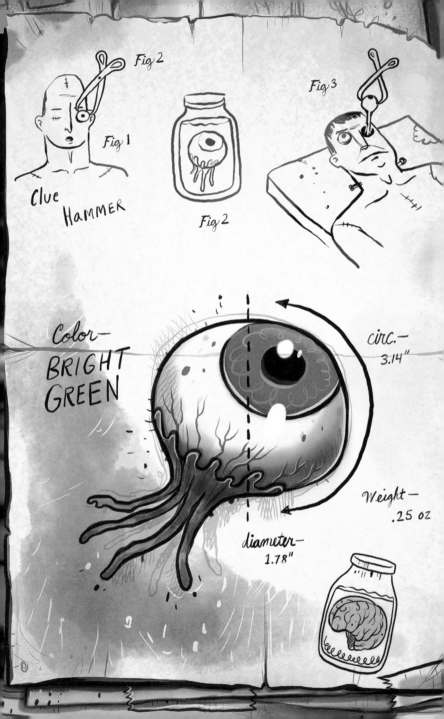